MAGICAL HORSES

By

CLEOPATRA EGYPT

Illustration by Cleopatra Egypt
and Raphael Reclusabo
Cover by John Long

First Printing
Published by
Cleopatra Egypt

Printed in the United States of America

FOR MY DAUGHTER
Shana Bourne

CONTENTS

ACKNOWLEDGMENTS

I thank my daughter, Shana Bourne, for constantly reading the story, proofreading it and suggesting ways to make it better.

I thank Nefertiti McNeill and Kiese Laymon for believing in the story and making suggestions for making it more interesting.

I thank John Long for supporting my vision.

INTRODUCTION

As a child growing up in Haiti during the 1960's and early '70's, I was fascinated by the culture of Haitian Vodou. Being in Vodou ceremonies involved the collective experience of song, dance, spirit possession and participating in the sharing of food with my peers and elders.

The spirits honored in Vodou are mythological figures that are part of the everyday lives of many Haitians living in Haiti and abroad. There are no written texts that I know of that present these myths in a dramatic story.

I have written *Magical Horses* to show the characteristics of the eight principle spirits in Haitian Vodou and to convey in a creative way the interaction between them.

MAGICAL HORSES

There was once a Haitian farmer named Azaka who had a large farm and always wore green. He never hired farmhands to help him with his chores. Instead his two horses, Ogou and Fréda, bore the burden of sowing the seeds for tomatoes, mangoes, and corn, planting yams and sugar canes, and harvesting those crops on his farm.

Ogou was the male horse, and Azaka always draped him in red. He rode him to the marketplace when he sold his merchandise. Fréda, the mare, whom he always draped in pink, helped him plow his field. Both horses worked very hard but were always hungry because Azaka only fed them once a day, early in the morning.

One day Azaka's best friend and Vodou priestess, Ezili Dantò, came to visit him at sunset, wearing a navy blue cotton dress that gleamed against her black skin. They went into the barn where the two horses were laying in the hay to do a vèvè honoring Legba, God of Crossroads. An oil lamp lit the room as Ezili Dantò used the hay on the ground to form the vèvè -- two overlapping crosses inside a circle. Once she finished, she kneeled on the ground and leaned forward to kiss the

1

vèvè three times. Azaka did the same. The horses looked on curiously as they listened to Ezili Dantò speak to Azaka, who was still kneeling on the ground.

"You must do this ritual every morning if you want to remain in this body and not turn back into a horse. Neglecting to honor Legba every day will lead to terrible consequences."

Upon hearing these words, Ogou and Fréda looked at each other, then quickly turned away so that Azaka and Ezili Dantò wouldn't see them listening as they pushed the door. When it opened, a sudden breeze came through, blowing all the hay around them and wiping out Legba's vèvè. Azaka turned to Ezili Dantò in amazement and quickly left the barn, overwhelmed by the presence of this powerful spirit. The door slammed shut; an eerie silence filled the barn. Left behind, Ezili Dantò stared curiously at Ogou and Fréda who were now boldly staring back at her. She looked searchingly into their eyes, wondering if they understood what had happened, and reluctantly left the barn. Ogou and Fréda walked over and quietly lay on the spot where the vèvè had been.

The next day it rained. When Azaka looked out his window and saw that it was raining, he went back to sleep and figured he would do the ritual and feed the horses later. As he lay in bed with his arms behind his head, he reflected. "I've remained a human being for forty years without doing this ridiculous vèvè for Legba. Nothing is going to happen. I'm not turning into a horse anytime soon. 'Terrible consequences?' There will be no terrible consequences. Dantò is always trying to scare me with these warnings. She was a horse, and I doubt that she does this vèvè everyday to remain a woman. Besides, we're more useful to Legba as humans than we are as horses. I'll do his vèvè and feed the horses on my own time."

Meanwhile, hungry for food, Ogou and Fréda complained to each other about how hard they worked and how little they had to eat. Ogou told her, "I'm so jealous of the people I see in the market place who walk around freely and do as they please. I would so very much like to be a human being instead of a horse. I'm tired of bearing the weight of Azaka's body on me."

Fréda agreed. Ogou continued, "At the marketplace, I see many women with the most beautiful dresses. You can be like them someday." Fréda became excited about the prospect of being transformed into a human being.

"How do we do it?" She anxiously asked him.

"I have a plan. We'll call on Legba like Ezili Dantò and Azaka did with the hay and maybe Legba can change us. He'll turn me into a man and I'll fight for justice."

Fréda thought his plan sounded promising. "I'll change into a woman and become the most beautiful and glamorous woman in Haiti. If Azaka was a horse and turned into a human being, so can we."

With their hooved feet the two of them started forming a Legba vèvè with the hay scattered around the barn. Just as they finished the second cross, the door of the barn flew open and as before, a cold breeze came through, blowing all the hay around them. This time, the vèvè remained. The wind blew the door shut and instead of silence, the spirit of Legba, with his deep, soothing voice began to speak. His authoritative presence filled the barn. "I have heard your deepest yearning. Do not despair, for I will tell you how to make your wishes come true." At that moment, two flies came buzzing behind Ogou and Fréda's ears. The two horses understood Legba's secret message. Just as the flies flew off, the two horses let out a loud, "Heee! Heeeee!" The door of the barn opened and Ogou and Fréda galloped through the doorway and out of the barn, heading to the seashore.

When they arrived at the beach, they looked up at the sun shining through the rain. As they gazed up at the sky, a large rainbow appeared. The rain stopped and the rainbow slowly mutated into a bright white cloud. Out of it emerged two long, intertwined cobras floating in the cloud as they shed their old skin to expose their new multicolored, rainbow-like coating. A light blue dolphin shot out of the ocean and caught the falling snakeskins with its mouth. As it moved at great speed, it glided through the air for hundreds of yards and swallowed the skin. It twisted in midair before finally falling into the water with a splash.

Ogou and Fréda looked on in amazement as the two cobras, both over twelve feet long, separated themselves from each other and leaped onto the two horses. The male wrapped itself around Ogou and the female wrapped itself around Fréda as a sparkling display of colors began flashing all around them. The colorful lights faded. The cobras disappeared. Ogou and Fréda transformed into two masses of colorful thick liquid that slowly swirled as their horse-shaped bodies began changing into organs, tissues, limbs and finally human beings.

Ogou became a dark handsome man with a red satin shirt and red pants. Fréda looked down at her beautiful brown skin and sparkly pink sequined dress. They looked at each other in disbelief, hugged, and started jumping up and down screaming, "We did it! We are human beings! We are free!"

Azaka finally got out of bed at two in the afternoon. He brushed his teeth, changed out of his pajamas, cooked and ate brunch. As he chewed on his food, he thought about what he was going to do for the day.

After finishing his meal and cleaning up, he left the main house and walked to the barn. When he opened the door, he saw the hay piled up in one corner across from him. He drew closer to the center of the barn and stared blankly at the new Legba vèvè. "How did it get there? I didn't do a vèvè this morning." He looked around the rest of the barn for a few seconds and realized what was missing. "My horses are gone!" His scream echoed through the barn as he rushed out, heading straight to Ezili Dantò's house.

On the way, he passed the seashore, noticing a small house made of sand in the distance. "Who would build a house made of sand?" He kept walking without stopping to inquire about who lived there. He soon reached the forest that led to the mountaintop where Ezili Dantò lives. Surrounded by tall and shady trees, he walked through one winding path after another.

Now sweaty and tired, he stopped to sit under a mango tree. As he wiped the sweat off his forehead with his green cotton handkerchief he heard the cooing of a mourning dove. He looked up at the tree above him. The bird took flight and landed right in front of him, continuing his plaintive "coo coooo, coo coooo."

"What are you grieving about?" Azaka asked the white bird with a swaying tail.

"I'm lonely and I need a friend," the dove answered.

"I'll be your friend if you help me find my horses." Azaka raised one eyebrow the way he often does when he's suspicious of someone.

"I can't help you get your horses back but I can give you clarity and intuition," the dove offered, flapping its wings. "These are priceless attributes in a man."

"What do I have to do to get those? I'm wise enough to know that one never gets anything for free in the spirit world."

"Do you know what spirit I am?" asked the dove teasingly, as he flew swiftly over Azaka's head.

"No. Which one are you?" Azaka asked as his eyes followed the bird's flight.

"I am Gran Bwa, Spirit of the Forest. I'm the one who helps your friend Ezili Dantò when she needs to know which leaves to work with for her powerful charms. I can also transform those in need of a ride to faraway places into one of my feathers to transport them where they want to go."

"I guess if I became your friend, in the future I wouldn't have to walk all this way to see her for her charms," Azaka said, unamused.

"You've got it. You're a smart fellow," Gran Bwa said, cocking his head to one side.

Azaka felt a request coming from Gran Bwa. "What's the catch? Tell me quickly. I have no time to waste. It will soon be sunset. And I want to be home by then." He adjusted his floppy green hat and stared at the dove expectantly.

"Tomorrow, I would like you to build me an altar made of wood and drape it in my spirit color, yellow. Then every morning when you get up, pour a libation with water in the four cardinal directions as you repeat my name three times. I also want you to place a fresh cup of coffee every morning on my altar." Azaka shifted his weight from one foot to another and clicked his tongue as he thought about this.

"That's a lot to ask for, Gran -- Gran. What's your name again?"

The dove opened his beak and let out an eerie chuckle. "Gran Bwa is my name. You should remember it. You will need me someday."

"I cannot and will not be a slave to you by doing these ridiculous rituals every day. I am a farmer. That is how I put food on my table and money in my pocket. Doing these rites will only make me feel like I'm bound to you." Azaka paused and stared straight into the bird's beady little eyes before adding, "And I don't want to do that."

" I thought you would show a bit of humility after your horses left you. Instead you are as arrogant as ever." And with that, the dove flew away.

Azaka searched for Gran Bwa but the bird was nowhere in sight. Stone-faced, he leaned back against the mango tree as a feeling of loneliness overcame him. "Those horses were my life." Feeling desperate, he flung his hat to the ground and started banging his head against the tree. He stepped away from the tree and stood in the middle of the pathway, tightening his coarse, veiny fists as if ready to fight. "One day of not doing that vèvè and everything falls apart. What will you do next, Legba?

Turn me back into a horse?" His voice was echoing through the forest as he continued to yell, "I will not be turned back into a horse! Never!" Once the echo had subsided, he sat back down quietly against the tree to collect his thoughts. A little while later, he stood up and continued walking with a new resolve: getting to Ezili Dantò's house as soon as possible.

The forest led to a series of hills that guided him to the mountaintop where Ezili Dantò lived. As he drew closer, the sound of beating drums filled the air. For a moment, he forgot about his horses and started dancing by himself in front of the house, swaying his small wiry frame to the beat of the drums. The man who was beating on the drums was Ezili Dantò's son, 18-year-old T-Jan.

T-Jan started making his way towards Azaka to welcome him but Ezili stepped out of her house and ran ahead of him so that she would be the first one he saw.

"Welcome my dear friend," she said, placing her soft hands on Azaka's face before hugging him. "I had a feeling you would be here today."

"Dantò, why do you live so far?" Azaka pulled away and looked at her. "Do you know how long I've been walking to get here?"

"Had you done the Legba vèvè like I instructed you to, you wouldn't have had to come all this way to solve your problems." Embarrassed, he looked down.

Ezili Dantò led him to the front porch of her small colorful house and sat him down on a bench. "Tell me, what happened?" Without hesitation, Azaka started recounting the story. Sitting next to Ezili Dantò, who was smoothing her flowery blue dress and swinging the porch bench with her feet, Azaka looked like a small child talking to his mother. After telling her about how he found out his horses were missing, Ezili Dantò looked perplexed.

"I wonder if they did it," she asked herself aloud.

"How could they?" Azaka responded, looking at her. "They're just horses."

"We were horses once too. Remember?" Ezili Dantò pursed her rounded lips and sucked her teeth. "I knew they were watching us yesterday."

"We should have done the vèvè somewhere else," Azaka reproached, shaking his head.

Dantò patted his leg roughly and rose from the bench. "Let's go inside and summon Danbala and Ayida Wèdo."

"Will they be able to tell us what happened to them?"

"I am certain of it. Let's go inside and start," she said, taking Azaka's hand and guiding him through the dim doorway into the house.

He followed her to her backyard filled with chickens, goats and black pigs. The two of them walked through a cemented hallway that led to a small cozy room painted in white. At the doorway was a brown doormat made of hemp. They took off their sandals and wiped their feet on it. Ezili Dantò entered first. Azaka remained at the doorway unnerved, as the room was filled with an aura of mystery. She motioned to him to come in and directed him to one of two chairs facing her altar at the center of the room.

Azaka stared blankly at the medium-sized table covered with a white embroidered tablecloth. His eyes wandered to the large Vodou flag above the altar, on which a rainbow was sewn with sequins. Ezili Dantò drew close to him to explain.

"Each one of these colors stand for a spirit, and we are among those spirits. The green is for the Spirit of the Fields, and that's you." She pointed her index finger at Azaka's color on the rainbow while he stared at the flag in concentration. "The white is for the Spirit of Transformation. That's Danbala and Ayida Wedo. The navy blue is for the Spirit of Motherhood. That's me. The light blue is for the Spirit of the Sea, the blue dolphin Agwé who gives us dreams and allows us to travel to other worlds in our sleep. The yellow is for the Spirit of the Forest, Gran Bwa. He gives clarity and intuition. He helps me come up with magic potions for my clients." Azaka grabbed Ezili Dantò's arm and burst out, "I met him on my way here!"

"You did? What did he tell you?" Azaka let go of her arm and hesitated. She quickly understood.

"That's between you and him. No need to tell me. Let's continue." She resumed her explanation. "The red is for the warrior. That's your horse, Ogou. The Pink is for the Spirit of Love. That's your horse, Fréda. And the purple is for the Spirit of Death, called Gédé." Feeling overwhelmed, Azaka took a deep breath and responded, "There's a lot to learn."

"In time you will learn, Azaka. You will." She patted his shoulder gently and smiled.

Ezili Dantò's attention now turned to the altar, where a wooden sculpture of two intertwined cobras had been placed in the center of the display. In front of it was a small plate of flour with an egg sitting in the middle. To the right of the wooden snakes was a bottle of Haitian rum. To the left of the sculpture rested a bowl of cornmeal and an ason (a multicolored rattle made of a gourd with a piece of wood attached to it to use as a handle). Azaka watched as she picked up the ason and started shaking it rhythmically to keep the rhythm of her song.

Legba nan baryè a
Legba ki mèt espri yo
Voyé Danbala Wèdo
Voyé Ayida Wèdo

Voyé yo palé avèk nou

Legba at the gate
Legba master of spirits
Send Danbala Wèdo
Send Ayida Wèdo
Send them to talk to us

After her first verse, T-Jan came in with his drum and joined in the singing. She handed the ason to Azaka, who reluctantly took it from her, looking to T-Jan for reassurance before continuing the rhythm as he shook the ason. Ezili Dantò picked up the bowl of cornmeal from the table and took a handful of it to draw a Legba vèvè on the floor in front of the altar. She sang louder, overpowering T-Jan's singing as he continued to beat on the drum and Azaka shook the ason.

Legba nan baryè a
Legba ki mèt espri yo
Voyé Danbala Wèdo
Voyé Ayida Wèdo

Voyé yo palé avèk nou

The Legba vèvè was now completed and the singing stopped. Ezili Dantò was calm and relaxed. She looked as if she was in a trance as she placed the bowl of cornmeal back on the altar. She picked up the bottle of rum to get ready for the libation. She began a new song before the libation, and T-Jan waited until he heard the whole song before resuming his drumming.

Danbala Wèdo mèt transfòmasyon
Ayida Wèdo métrès transfòmasyon
Danbala Wèdo, Ayida Wèdo
Vin palé avèk nou o, Fè nou konnen sak pasé
Fè nou konnen sak pasé o, Fè nou konnen sak pasé

Danbala Wèdo, master of transformation
Ayida Wèdo, master of transformation
Danbala Wèdo, Ayida Wèdo
Come and speak to us o
Let us know what happened

Let us know what happened o
Let us know what happened

T-Jan was now drumming with more enthusiasm. Accustomed to his mother's rituals, he felt a revelation about to take place. Drawing from T-Jan's energy, Azaka shook the ason with excitement and started to sing along with T-Jan and Ezili Dantò.

Ezili Dantò did the libation as she sang, pouring the rum and curtsying in the four directions. First she poured north, then south, then east and finally west as she splashed the rum all over the cornmeal. She put the bottle back on the altar, walked over to Azaka and sat next to him as she continued to sing. The singing got louder and more intense as Azaka and T-Jan joined in while clapping rhythmically.

Danbala Wèdo mèt transfòmasyon
Ayida Wèdo métrès transfòmasyon
Danbala Wèdo, Ayida Wèdo
Vin palé avèk nou o, Fè nou konnen sak pasé
Fè nou konnen sak pasé o, Fè nou konnen sak pasé

Suddenly, a misty fog filled the room. T-Jan stopped the drumming and singing. Ezili Dantò and T-Jan were quiet. All eyes were on the eerie cloud above them. Azaka gasped as he looked up and saw two long intertwined cobras floating in the cloud as they shed their old skin to expose their colorful coating.

Everyone looked on in amazement at the transformation of Ogou and Fréda from two separate liquid masses, into organs, tissues, limbs and finally human beings. Struck by Fréda's beauty, Azaka cried out, "Fréda!" Ezili Dantò turned to him, stunned by his outburst. Azaka reached out for Ezili Dantò's hand and she held it tightly. They all watched, dumbfounded, as the misty fog began to dissipate. After the room finally cleared, Azaka walked over to the altar alone and put his face in his hands.

"I don't believe it," he whispered to himself. He fought to maintain his composure, but Ezili could see his face beginning to break. She walked over to him and laid a hand gently on his shoulder.

"They have become like us," she said, looking down at the altar and closing her eyes. For a moment they both remained lost in their thoughts. Ezili turned to Azaka to comfort him. "You have to let them go and move on with your life. Go back and start a new farm. Have a bountiful harvest. Hire farmhands. Pay them a decent wage and send them to sell your goods for you at the marketplace. Don't try to do it all yourself."

"I'm going to have less than I did before!" Azaka yelped, flinging his arms up in despair. "I will become a poor man."

"No! You will have more. The more you share, the more you'll receive."

Azaka shrugged her hand off his shoulder and rolled his eyes. "Dantò, I will have to spend a lot more to get these results that you're speaking of."

"That's the trouble with you Azaka." Ezili snapped as she walked over to her chair. "You are a penny-pincher." He looked down and seemed to accept that there was truth to Dantò's words. There always was.

He looked up at her with big pleading eyes. "I need someone that I can trust to help me get started."

"I can spare you my son for a while. With his drumming, he will attract a lot of people to your farm. He's very useful to me in my spirit work, but I will spare him. Pay him well."

"I will pay him well. I promise." Azaka squeezed his friend's hand tightly, adjusted his hat and began to leave.

Ezili Dantò grabbed him by the arm. "Aren't you forgetting something?"

"Oh, yes," he answered blankly, almost as if he was hoping she would forget. "How much do I owe you?"

"That will be 300 gourds."

He reached in his back pocket and pulled out his wallet. He counted the money and handed it to her. "Thank you," she answered in satisfaction. "Now I will get T-Jan."

Not long afterwards, T-Jan and Azaka started out to Azaka's farm before sunset. Azaka told T-Jan about Gran Bwa and asked him if he had his own spirit who looked out for him. T-Jan told him that for him it was his mother's spirit that guided him. She's the one who made sure that he learned all the rhythms for the different spirits so that he would be able to summon them for her clients. Azaka asked him if he knew the rhythm for Gran Bwa. He told him he did.

"Why? Do you want me to summon him for you?" asked T-Jan.

"Yes. Since you're here, I want to see if he'll tell me where to find Ogou and Fréda," Azaka told him.

"Sure. I'll call him for you." T-Jan immediately started drumming Gran Bwa's rhythm, and broke into song.

Gran Bwa ki moun ou ye
Gran Bwa ki moun ou ye
Ou pwomèt li konesans
Gran Bwa o
Gran Bwa ki moun ou ye
Gran Bwa ki moun ou ye
Ou pwomèt li konesans
Gran Bwa o

Gran Bwa a who are you?

Gran Bwa a who are you?
You did promise him wisdom
Gran Bwa o
Gran Bwa a who are you?
Gran Bwa a who are you?
You did promise him wisdom
Gran Bwa o

Just as T-Jan finished singing, Azaka saw Gran Bwa fly above his head. Azaka screamed out, "Here he is! Here he is!"

"Yes. Gran Bwa heard you," T-Jan said.

As soon as Gran Bwa flew away, Azaka became excited and suddenly full of ideas. "Let's hurry and make it to the beach by sunset. Gran Bwa has just given me an intuition about where to find them."

They moved swiftly through the woods. T-Jan and Azaka arrived at the beach and drew closer to the house made of sand, hesitating for a moment to listen for any sound coming from the house. They heard nothing. Azaka rushed inside. T-Jan followed him as he struggled to keep his drum strapped to his back. They had both been walking for a long time, and all T-Jan wanted to do now is rest, but Azaka felt differently. He was anxious to follow his hunch and see if Fréda and Ogou were living in the house made of sand.

They stepped in the doorway and Azaka's eyes immediately darted to the four corners of the small room, looking for the tall figures of a man and woman. He saw nothing but two wooden beds with bare mattresses inside. Disappointed, Azaka sat on the bed in the front room.

"This intuition given to me by Gran Bwa didn't pan out. I came here certain that I would find Ogou and Fréda but they don't even live here. So much for Gran Bwa working for me."

T-Jan told him comfortingly, "My mother always said that it is we who work for the spirits and not the other way around. She said that life is a gift they've given to us. For that, we should do special favors for them."

"To think that Gran Bwa demanded that I make him an altar tomorrow. I'm not doing any such thing." Azaka nodded his head in agreement and stretched on the bed for a nap. T-Jan walked to the back room, climbed on the bed and also went to sleep.

At sunset, while Azaka and T-Jan were sleeping, Agwé, the light blue dolphin with a streamlined body and a crisscross pattern on his side, emerged from the ocean, poking his head out from under the water. He had a long beak and at the center of his forehead was the black outline of a mystical looking eye. Agwé looked towards the cliff across from him in search of Fréda. He leaped out of the water and started making a spectacular whistling sound, then plunged back under.

Fréda heard him as she approached the small cliff wearing a pink bathing suit with glittering sequins. She climbed up the cliff and stood on top of a large rock ready to dive into the ocean below. Again, Agwé leaped out of the water. Fréda jumped for a dive, and Agwé and Fréda plunged together into the water with a big splash. They swam alongside each other for a while, and then started swimming in graceful arcs across each other like two well-coordinated dancers, forming a circle. Agwé hurled himself sideways into the air. Fréda flung herself over Agwé. Together they overlapped, forming the shape of an X that signifies the strength of the bond they share even though they came from two different worlds. They continued their dance in a spiraling curve, forming a continuous figure eight that expressed the infinite nature of their friendship.

Across them, Ogou stood on the beach clapping, mesmerized by the dance. When Agwé plunged into the water, Fréda followed him down under. Ogou waited for her to come back up. She never did. After awhile, he grew restless and started calling her name. Still she never surfaced.

Back in the house made of sand, Azaka woke up and walked over to the back room to awaken T-Jan who was already pacing around the room, restless and ready to go.

"Tomorrow we're going to get farm hands for cheap labor and you're going to help me." Azaka told him decidedly. He kicked T-Jan's foot slightly and told him, "Let's go and get things ready for the morning."

Azaka and T-Jan left the house and made their way towards the seashore as they continued their way to the farm. Ten feet away from the house, they heard Ogou calling out, "Fréda! Come back up! Fréda!" T-Jan immediately ran towards the voice. Azaka sped after him, urging him to ignore Ogou's cry.

"Don't go there! I know another way home."

"I think it's Ogou. He sounds like he needs our help," T-Jan pressed on.

"It's dark and scary. Come with me. Let the spirits who transformed them help them," Azaka said as he quickly whisked him off the beach. Ogou's cry lingered faintly in the distance. Overwhelmed with guilt, T-Jan kept looking back behind him.

"We should have stopped to help him. Maybe Fréda is drowning." He glanced over at Azaka with a look of disappointment.

"When you return home, your mother can summon Danbala and Ayida Wedo and they'll give her a vision that will show her what happened to them. Better yet, if you play Ogou's rhythm, then Fréda's with your drum, they'll be drawn to my farm and work for me again," Azaka told him.

"Work for you? But they're free now," T-Jan retorted.

"They're free but they have nothing. What will they eat? Where will they sleep? You heard Ogou. He's in trouble, and he's going to need me. When Legba turned me into a human being, I had nothing either."

"He gave you farming skills, didn't he?"

"He did, but first I started out working for those who had more than me, and I earned very little. I saved all the money I had until I bought my piece of land. I started at the bottom, " Azaka kicked at the sand with one foot to emphasize this point.

"I hope Ogou and Fréda have special skills like you do."

"I hope so too but I wouldn't count on it," he scoffed. "The spirits don't give anything for free."

They arrived at the farm. Azaka stood by the barn as T-Jan went on challenging him for answers.

"What have you given Legba in return for the good luck he's brought you, Azaka?"

"I housed and fed the horses that he left in my care, didn't I?"

T-Jan put a hand on his hip and saw Azaka's disapproving look. "Is that why they ran away?"

Angry, Azaka pulled T-Jan by the collar of his blue denim shirt.

"Listen T-Jan, you're getting on my last nerve with all your questions. Just because your mother is a priestess doesn't mean you can come here and disrespect me on my own farm."

T-Jan pushed him away and continued to confront him. "I heard about how you treated these horses. I'm not going to let you take advantage of me again. I want to know right now how much you're going to pay me for my services."

Azaka started screaming at him in frustration. "You're a drummer T-Jan, not a farmer! How much use can you really be to me?" Azaka slammed his fist on the door of the barn authoritatively. "Sleep where the horses slept. I will speak with you tomorrow."

T-Jan watched Azaka leave. He felt dejected and wondered what he had gotten himself into. He turned to face the door, leaning his forehead on it for a moment, then slowly turned the knob to the barn and opened it. When he walked in he noticed the oil lamp at the corner of the room and started searching on the floor for matches. Having found them, he lit the lamp and held it to guide him around the barn. He smiled as he stared amusedly at the Legba vèvè. "Very clever horses," he reflected. He bent down, slumped to the ground and placed his head on the Legba vèvè made of hay. As soon as he rested on the hay, he felt a sense of comfort and peace and broke into song.

Mwen vini pou m ede w
M mande w fè pri avèk mwen
Ou pa di m anyen
Ou pa di m anyen
A p gen jistis yon jou, Azaka veye zo w
veye zo w, veye zo w, Azaka veye zo w

I have come to help you
And asked you to settle
You have told me nothing
You have told me nothing
There'll be justice one day
Azaka wa atch out
watch out

watch out

Azaka wa atch out

Drawing strength from the song's words, he got up, grabbed his drum and started beating the rhythm of the song as he sang:

Mwen vini pou m ede w

M mande w fè pri avèk mwen

Ou pa di m anyen

Ou pa di m anyen

A p gen jistis yon jou, Azaka veye zo w

veye zo w, veye zo w, Azaka veye zo w

He stopped singing and drumming to gather his thoughts. With the song still on his mind, he started humming its last verse. As soon as he had finished humming "Azaka veye zo w" for a second time, he rushed out of the barn and headed back to the beach.

T-Jan hurried to the shore with his drum and the oil lamp. As he got closer to the ocean, Ogou was still calling out Fréda's name, pleading for her to come to the surface. He ran to Ogou. As he got nearer Ogou quickly said, "My friend, Fréda was dancing with the blue dolphin, Agwé, and when they finished, she dove into the ocean and never came back up."

T-Jan told him reassuringly, "Do not worry. I know that she is the Spirit of Love. I will play her rhythm and if she's alive, she'll return." He immediately started playing her beat as he broke into song:

Fréda, Agwé rele w

Fréda, Agwé rele w

Poko kite nou

Fréda, Agwé rele w

Poko kite nou

Mwen konnen Agwé bezwen w

Mwen konnen Agwé bezwen w

Poko kite nou

Mwen konnen Agwé rele w

Mwen konnen Agwé bezwen w

Poko kite nou

Fréda, Agwé has called
Fréda, Agwé has called

Do not leave us

Fréda, Agwé has called

Do not leave us

I know Agwé needs you

I know Agwé needs you

Do not leave us

I know Agwé has called

I know Agwé needs you

Do not leave us

Before long, Fréda shot back up from the water without Agwé and started swimming to shore.

Ogou ran towards her with his arms outstretched as she got out of the water. She hugged him and looked surprised to see T-Jan. Ogou was excited, "Fréda, you're back. Thank Legba, you're back." He turned to T-Jan, "Thank you."

T-Jan took the opportunity to introduce himself, "T-Jan is my name. I'm the son of Ezili Dantò, the Spirit of Motherhood. Azaka came to see my mother to find out what happened to you both." The joyous mood quickly changed as soon as T-Jan mentioned Azaka's name.

"Did he send you here to take us back to his farm and work for him like slaves?" Ogou asked angrily.

"Ogou, do not jump to conclusions. We're humans now. We don't have to do anything we don't want to," Fréda told him.

"We damn well better not," Ogou snapped.

"Let's go back to the House Made of Sand. Agwé told me he's left some things for us," Fréda said.

Ogou and T-Jan followed her. When they arrived at the house, the front room was filled with basic necessities that were not there before. T-Jan was stunned. Ogou and Fréda rummaged through the towels, sheets and new cotton clothing for Ogou and Fréda in their spirit colors. They also noticed the two oil lamps and three chairs that were not there before. Fréda took a pink towel and pink cotton dress and went into the bathroom to shower and change. Ogou remained in the front room and sat on one of the chairs, thanking T-Jan for playing the rhythm that brought Fréda back up. After

Fréda finished changing she returned to the front room and sat down.

"Agwé did all this, Fréda?" Ogou asked in amazement.

"Yes. And there's more I have to tell you," she replied, smoothing her dress on her lap.

"It's a good thing this room didn't look like this when Azaka and I were here earlier," T-Jan remarked.

"Azaka was here? What was he doing here? What did he want?" Ogou yelled, shooting up from his seat.

"Relax, Ogou!" Fréda scolded, giving him a dirty look that seemed to return him to his senses. "He can't hurt you. Let's all sit down. We have many things to talk about."

T-Jan turned to them both with genuine concern. "He left thinking that neither of you live here."

"He can't harm us. Agwé told me so. Besides, we can't go on avoiding him forever," Fréda said, looking at Ogou reassuringly.

"My mother sent me to help him get his farm running again. I'm supposed to draw people to it through my drumming, but the man is so mean spirited, selfish and arrogant that I can't stand being around him anymore," T-Jan said, throwing up his hands.

"I understand," Fréda told T-Jan, patting him gently on his knee.

"Try and have him sit on you half the day and see how you really can't tolerate him," Ogou said.

"Do you know that he left me in the barn to sleep? He didn't even offer me a bed. I'm here to help him and he treats me like an animal," T-Jan said, immediately realizing his slip. He tried to make amends. "Pardon me, but not even animals should be treated that way."

"We were once there," Ogou said pensively.

For a moment all three remained silent, each lost in their own thoughts as they gazed at the gifts on the beds. Ogou looked T-Jan straight in the eye, "We have to teach him a lesson, one that will hurt him as much as he hurt us."

"We should," T-Jan agreed.

"But revenge only leads to violence and violence leads to more violence," Fréda said.

"You know, ever since I turned into a man, I've been remembering things from my past life as a horse for Toussaint Louverture," Ogou replied.

"You were a horse for Toussaint Louverture, the liberator who led the Haitian revolution?" T-Jan asked excitedly.

"I was. Before Toussaint liberated Haiti there was the Night of Fire that started it all," Ogou said, as his eyes glimmered and he glanced at Fréda mischievously.

"Are you implying that we should replicate the Night of Fire and burn his farm?"

"Maybe," Ogou said to her.

"We should not even think about that. We need a place where we can work and earn a living. Agwé is not going to shower us with gifts forever," Fréda said.

"He probably wouldn't pay you very much. I asked him how much he was going to pay me for my services, and he refused to answer me. Instead he put me down and told me that I wouldn't be much use to him as a drummer," T-Jan told them. If we have to go back and work on his farm, we have to know how to farm. You shouldn't take what he said too harshly. He's only being practical," Fréda said.

Ogou turned and faced Fréda. "Speak for yourself. I'm not going back to his farm."

"After I did the Legba Dance with Agwé, and went under the ocean with him he made a request of me."

T-Jan and Ogou leaned towards her to listen intently. "What did he ask you to do?" Ogou asked.

Fréda hesitated. "It's not that he asked me to do anything..."

"Go on," T-Jan said anxiously.

"He told me that if I did the Legba Dance with at least 32 people, Azaka would change into a better person," Fréda said. She got up and slowly paced around the room as she continued to speak like a prophet with an important message. "That's why it's important for us to go back there. We should bring all kinds of people to his farm and get them to dance."

"I don't know if it's going to work Fréda. He's not a receptive man," T-Jan said.

Ogou nodded his head in agreement. Fréda sat back down and resumed speaking with an authoritative tone. "You should go back to the barn and pretend you never left. When Azaka wakes up in the morning, tell him that you'll look for us if he wishes you to. If he agrees, when you come back we'll go to the farm with you."

Ogou angrily got up from his chair. "And then what? Work like a slave as we did before, with very little to eat? I won't have it! I would rather die than go back and live under those conditions. I didn't turn into a human being to be Azaka's slave!" He quickly ran out.

Fréda looked stunned. "I've never seen him this angry before."

"I'll go talk to him." T-Jan assured her before rushing out of the house.

He ran after Ogou who was now quite a distance from the House Made of Sand. "Ogou, wait! Where are you rushing to?" T-Jan yelled.

"I know where to go to destroy Azaka. I'm going to the cemetery to see Gédé," Ogou told him.

"Gédé is the Spirit of Death. He ends things by scaring people off with his rara band. He doesn't do anything for anyone unless they form a contract with him," T-Jan said. "Don't go see him unless you're willing to give up something."

Ogou breaks down and tells him, "I've been feeling lost since I turned into a man. I feel no sense of belonging. If Gédé wants to make me a part of his circle, so be it."

Ogou left. T-Jan remained still as he pondered Ogou's words. He understood all too well Ogou's feelings because he himself didn't know much about the world outside his mother's circle. Not long after, he returned to the House Made of Sand to tell Fréda about Ogou.

Ogou arrived at the cemetery, which was filled with crosses on tombstones. He stood by one of them and started singing:

Gédé Gédé, Azaka derespekte m
Gédé Gédé, Azaka derespekte m
Mwen vini pou m fè revanj
fè revanj, fè revanj
Mwen vini pou m fè revanj
Gédé Gédé, Azaka derespekte m

Gédé Gédé, Azaka disrespected me
Gédé Gédé, Azaka disrespected me
I have come to do revenge
do revenge, do revenge
I have come to do revenge
Gédé Gédé, Azaka disrespected me

Just as he finished singing, a band of sixteen men emerged, running forward. They were dressed in colorful, sequined satin shirts and matching knee-length pants. Ribbons were hanging from their hats and waist as they played and danced to the fast-paced rhythm called the banda. Seven of them were playing bamboo instruments called vaksins. Another three were beating on goatskin drums. Gédé, a slender, dark-skinned man with a patch on one eye rushed to the front of the band with his baton to show off his moves. He was dressed in black satin pants and a silk purple shirt. He danced with his knees bent and his hips undulating as he threw the baton in the air then passed it across his back. He stopped when he came face to face with Ogou. "Have you come here to see me for revenge against Azaka?" Gede asked Ogou.

"Yes, Gédé. I need you and your band to help me seize Azaka's farm so that I can take it for myself and start a new farm. I can hire farmhands, grow more vegetables and share the profits that I'll make with them," Ogou explained.

"Don't you know it's against the law to steal another man's land? Just because I'm the spirit of death doesn't mean I go around hurting people," Gédé responded with sarcasm.

"You inspired many rebellions in your lifetime. You, the Spirit of Death, the one who puts an end to old things to give rise to new beginnings," Ogou said.

"Putting an end to old ways that aren't working doesn't necessarily have to happen by theft or violence," Gédé said.

"You were at the Alligator Woods. Bookman was possessed by you and you urged him to lead the revolt that brought on the Night of Fire," Ogou reminisced.

"Were you there too?" Gédé asked, amazed by Ogou's recollection.

"I was with Toussaint. I did the best I could for him during the revolution. As his horse, I gave him access to a lot of places where many people couldn't enter. We talked many times," Ogou recollected.

"In the end you failed him," Gédé retorted.

"There's nothing I could have done to keep him from falling into the trap of the French who took him to France to die in a cold prison. I was stuck in the body of a horse," Ogou said sadly.

"So, now that you're a man you can't wait to show your muscle against a man that you see as powerful," Gédé remarked.

"He sees me as a servant and not his equal," Ogou told him.

"I've heard of Azaka's arrogance, and I guess he can use a lesson in humility. But before I do you this favor, you'll have to pledge that you'll be part of my rara band during the rara season," Gédé demanded.

"When is the rara season?" Ogou asked.

"It's the forty days from Ash Wednesday to Easter. We start playing music and dancing from the eve of Lent and continue to go around different neighborhoods for six weeks until Easter week. Can you pledge that you'll be with us?" Gédé asked him.

"I do," Ogou agreed.

"Good. Since you agree to be part of our circle, I'll tell you what I can do," Gédé said. "We will scare him by gathering what will seem like a large army against him. There will be no violence, but I have the power to change things. Legba may give life but I have the power to transform it," Gédé said resolutely.

"What do you mean?" Ogou asked.

"How soon would you like to go to Azaka's farm?" Gédé asked impatiently.

"The sooner, the better," Ogou said, decidedly.

"Then, we shall go now," Gédé concluded.

The rara band resumed playing their fast-paced banda music as they danced out of the cemetery towards the different crossroads that led to Azaka's farm. People on porches of the houses that lined the roads watched the band. Many others joined in the rara after listening to Gédé singing:

Espri mò a nan vil la

Espri mò a nan vil la

Reini pou nou detwi Azaka Azaka

Reini pou nou detwi Azaka

Death spirit is here

Death spirit is here

Reunite to destroy Azaka Azaka

Reunite to destroy Azaka

Gédé sang the song over and over as the band accompanied him. The crowd that followed the band had now grown to thirty-two. They moved swiftly from crossroad to crossroad like an army ready for action.

Meanwhile, Fréda and T-Jan took a short cut to Azaka's farm to arrive there before the rara band, which they could hear in the distance. They finally arrived at the farm and knocked on Azaka's door. Azaka woke up with his pajamas on, half asleep, and opened the door. Azaka was taken aback by Fréda's presence and remained speechless. T-Jan wasted no time in playing the rhythm to Fréda's song:

Se Ezili Fréda m ye

Se Ezili Fréda m ye
Kouzen Zaka Agwé voye m
pou m veye zo w
veye zo w
Kouzen Zaka Agwé voye m
pou m veye zo w

I am Ezili Fréda
I am Ezili Fréda
Cousin Zaka Agwé has sent me
To watch your back
watch your back
Cousin Zaka Agwé has sent me
to watch your back

Just as Azaka was motioning to them to come in, the overbearing sound of Gédé's song and the rara band drawing near filled Azaka's house. Azaka quickly pulled Fréda and T-Jan inside and closed the door behind them. Azaka's eyes were bulging with fear, "It's Gédé and his rara band. They're coming for me. Why? What did I do?" Azaka asked nervously. T-Jan tried to explain,

"Ogou was insulted because you expected him to work on your farm again for very little pay. So, he went to Gédé."

"What are they going to do to me?" Azaka asked with his feet trembling.

Fréda interjected, "Don't be afraid. Let's go out and face them."

Just as she uttered these words, the rara band stood in front of Azaka's house with the music blasting. Fréda opened the door. Gédé turned to motion to the musicians to stop playing and the music stopped. Fréda boldy faced Gédé, Ogou and the crowd. "My name is Fréda. Have you come here to dance with us?" Gédé responded to her invitation, "With a woman as beautiful as you are it would be my pleasure."

Ogou nudged Gédé to get him to focus on the reason why they came and told Azaka, "We have come for you, Azaka. Your time on this farm is up." Nervous, Azaka apologized, "If I've offended you by thinking you could work for me again, I'm sorry." Ogou was filled with anger.

"You treated me like garbage." He turned to Fréda, "Speak up Fréda. You know how badly he treated us."

Fréda stepped forward to address the crowd. "I am very happy that you are all here because I'd like to share with you a magical dance that Agwé, the Spirit of the Sea has taught me."

Ogou interrupted, "Fréda, this is not a time for idealism."

Gédé interjected, "Let her speak, Ogou."

Fréda went on, "This dance is a tool for the practice of collective collaboration. When done with at least 32 of you, dancers come from four directions to meet at the center to form the pattern of a crossroad. This crossroad is a point where we come together to cross each other's path to create a common goal." Many in the crowd nodded in agreement. Smitten by her charm, Gédé asked, "What is this dance called, Fréda?" Fréda answered with enthusiasm, "It's called the Legba Dance. It will help us feel connected and set the stage for all our voices to be heard because in real communication each person contributes to a vision that can be realized when everyone actively participates.

T-Jan started beating his drum to the rhythm of the Legba Dance. The other drummers in the crowd put their drums down. The vaksin players laid their bamboo instruments on the ground, and the crowd formed a circle around Fréda. Azaka, Gédé and Ogou remained shocked by the effect of Fréda's speech and subsequently found themselves inside the circle with T-Jan and Fréda.

Fréda slowly demonstrated her dance to Azaka and Gédé. Ogou stepped aside to observe. Before long the crowd started imitating their every move. Soon, Fréda instructed them to line up and formed two vertical parallel lines. They danced in unison as they performed a series of steps and elegant hand movements. The two vertical lines changed to two horizontal lines, then a circle. As the group of more than sixteen dancers on each side moved out of the circle, they crossed each other's path and formed an X, signifying a crossroad. The dance continued in a spiraling curve, forming the symbol of infinity before the dancers formed the two vertical lines once more and started the dance all over again.

After repeating the Legba Dance four more times, everyone but Fréda got tired. Ogou stood untouched. They all sat in a circle around her. She gazed over the men and women and smiled. Feeling content, she told them, "My brothers and sisters, let's communicate to reach a common goal."

Azaka got up and ran back to the middle of the circle. "What common goal, Fréda? This is my farm, not yours." Seeing Azaka's confrontational mood, the crowd quickly got up. Fréda blushed with embarrassment. " I know it's your farm, but…"

"But what?" Azaka asked.

"I was trying to help you," Fréda bashfully responded.

"Go away, Fréda. I can deal with this on my own," Azaka retorted, thinking that the crowd had been appeased.

A man in the crowd shouted, "We need jobs. Can you hire us?" Annoyed, Azaka answered in a stern voice, "There's nothing I can do for you, brother. I have a very small farm. Leave at once." He then screamed at the top of his lungs, "All of you! Leave, now!"

The crowd moaned in disappointment. An angry man yelled out, "You have a lot of land here. There's a lot you can plant to make money and share with us."

"I'll say it again. I'm not in the business of creating jobs for people," Azaka told him fiercely.

Gédé was eying Azaka with deep scrutiny as he realized why Ogou was so mad at him. Inflamed, Ogou stepped to the center with a box of matches and asked, "Whom among you wants to help me burn this place? You heard what he said. He has no common goal to work for. Let's burn this farm!" Ogou ran toward the field. The crowd followed him yelling and screaming, "Burn this farm! Burn it! Burn it!" As Ogou ran past tree after tree, he lit one match after another and dropped them on dry leaves. The crowd took burning branches and spread the fire on the plants throughout the farm.

Azaka remained where he was, numb in disbelief. Gédé came face to face with him. As Gédé's fiery eyes stared at him, Gran Bwa, the bird, flew over Azaka's head saying, "I told you you would need me. I told you."

"Now, I'm going to transform you back to what you were." Gédé overwhelmed Azaka with his long arms. But as Gédé was raising his arms to begin the transformation, Gran Bwa flew by Azaka's ear and whispered, "Run for your life, run." Azaka took off in great speed. Gédé ran after him. They passed by Fréda and T-Jan who were standing side by side watching the fields of Azaka's farm go up in thick billowy flames.

Not satisfied with the burning field, Ogou led the mob to Azaka's house and set that on fire. As Fréda watched Ogou and the mob scream and jump for joy around the burning house, she remembered the conversation she had had days earlier with Ogou and T-Jan. That day she told them what Agwé had told her: "If you do the Legba Dance with at least 32 people, Azaka will change." At that moment, her faith in Agwé had gone.

Azaka ran through one crossroad after another as Gran Bwa flew overhead leading the way. Gédé followed them as fast as he could. Finally, Gran Bwa led Azaka to the forest. When Gédé saw Azaka and Gran Bwa enter the forest, he stopped. This was not his turf, and he knew of Gran Bwa's power to transform things as well.

Seeing that Gédé was no longer running after him, Azaka finally stopped to rest under the mango tree. Gran Bwa landed in front of him with his swaying tail, "Now, what are you going to do, my friend?"

Azaka was exhausted and scared. There were many thoughts running through his mind at once. "What do I do? What do I do?" He asked Gran Bwa furiously.

Gran Bwa told him, "I can hear your thoughts Azaka. And from what I see, you have no choice but to let me turn you into one of my feathers and take you to a faraway place where you can start over."

"A feather?" Azaka asked, surprised.

"Yes, a feather. That's the only way I can protect you. Gédé didn't come here tonight, but it's only a matter of time before he musters enough courage to come looking for you with his posse. I certainly can't carry you on my back as you are now. You have to change into a feather," Gran Bwa insisted.

"I don't want to change into a feather. I want to remain as I am. If I change now, there's no telling when you'll transform me into a human being again," Azaka told him.

Gran Bwa gave him an ultimatum. "It's either you change into a feather or you're on your own when Gédé, Ogou and the mob come looking for you."

"I don't seem to have a choice, do I?" Azaka asked.

"You'll have to trust me now, won't you?" Gran Bwa asked him sarcastically.

"I guess," Azaka told him sadly.

"After you agree to change, I'll turn you into a green feather on my back, and I'll take you to a new farm at sunrise tomorrow."

Reflecting, Azaka thought, "If only I had agreed to grant his request when he had asked me to, he would have given me intuition. I would have foreseen this. I have no choice but to believe that he'll set me free when we get to where he takes me."

"Are you ready?" Gran Bwa asked.

"I'm ready," Azaka responded.

Gran Bwa flapped its wings three times, then flew over Aaka and landed on his head. A large misty cloud emanated from beneath his tail feathers and surrounded the Spirit of the Field. Azaka's heart was beating very

54

fast. He let out a loud cry but it was too late. Gran Bwa flew to the top of the mango tree to observe Azaka's body spin over and over as it melted and merged with the mist. The mixture changed to a floating green feather that slowly glided towards the Spirit of the Forest and finally anchored itself on Gran Bwa's back.

As soon as he felt the new feather on his back, Gran Bwa became elated and started dancing from tree to tree in a flying frenzy. He started making plans.

"Tomorrow I'm going to visit Ogou, Ezili Fréda, Ezili Dantò and even Gédé to show off my green feather. I'll show them that I'm the most interesting bird in Haiti because I have a spirit on my back. I'm afraid we'll be with each other for a very long time, Azaka."

PRONUNCIATION OF CHARACTERS

Agwé	agwë
Azaka	äzäkä
Danbala	DAN-bala
Ezili Dantò	Èzili dantow
Ezili Fréda	Èzili frëda
Gédé	gëdë
Gran Bwa	GRAN-bwa
Ogou	ogou
Legba	leg-bä

RECOMMENDED BOOKS

Cosentino, Donald. Sacred Arts of Haitian Vodou. Los Angeles, CA: UCLA Fowler Museum of Cultural History, 1995.

Deren, Maya. Divine Horsemen: The Living Gods of Haiti. Kingston, NY: McPherson and Co., 1953.

Dubois, Laurent. Avengers of the New World: The Story of the Haitian Revolution. Cambridge, MA: Belknap Press of Harvard University Press, 2004.

Dunham, Katherine. Island Possessed. New York: Doubleday and Co., 1969.

Fleurant, Gerdes. Dancing Spirits: Rhythms and Rituals of Haitian Vodou, the Rada Rite. Westport, Ct.: Greenwood Publishing Group, Inc., 1996.

Gray, John Gray. Ashe, Traditional Religion and Healing in Sub-Saharan Africa and the Diaspora: A Classified International Bibliography: Westport, CT: Greenwood Press, 1989.

McAlister, Elizabeth. Rara! California: University of California Press, 2002.

Ott, Thomas. The Haitian Revolution, 1789-1804. Tennessee: University of Tennessee Press, 1973.

Roumain, Jacques. "Guinea," translated by Langston Hughes. In: The Langston Hughes Reader. New York, NY: George Braziller, Inc., 1958.

Wilcken, Lois Wilcken. The Drums of Vodou. Tempe, AZ: White Cliffs Media Co, 1992.

Wolkstein, Diane. The Magic Orange Tree and Other Haitian Folktales. New York, NY: Schocken Books, 1997.

MUSIC

Address of a Haitian record store: Marc Records, 1020 Rutland Road, Brooklyn, NY 11212. Phone: (718) 773-9507.

Names of some Haitian music groups: Bookman Eksperyans, Zin, Ram, Frisner Augustin & La Troupe Makandal.

ABOUT THE AUTHOR

Cleopatra Egypt was born in Port-au-Prince, Haiti in 1961. She immigrated to Brooklyn, New York with her parents and siblings at the age of eleven. She currently lives in Manhattan.